Dear Parent:
Your child's love of readi starts here!

Every child learns to read in a different [way] [and at his or her own]
speed. Some go back and forth between [each level and read their]
favorite books again and again. Others re[ad] [through each level in]
order. You can help your young reader improve and become more
confident by encouraging his or her own interests and abilities. From
books your child reads with you to the first books he or she reads
alone, there are I Can Read Books for every stage of reading:

SHARED READING
Basic language, word repetition, and whimsical illustrations,
ideal for sharing with your emergent reader

BEGINNING READING
Short sentences, familiar words, and simple concepts
for children eager to read on their own

READING WITH HELP
Engaging stories, longer sentences, and language play
for developing readers

READING ALONE
Complex plots, challenging vocabulary, and high-interest topics
for the independent reader

ADVANCED READING
Short paragraphs, chapters, and exciting themes
for the perfect bridge to chapter books

I Can Read Books have introduced children to the joy of reading
since 1957. Featuring award-winning authors and illustrators and a
fabulous cast of beloved characters, I Can Read Books set the
standard for beginning readers.

A lifetime of discovery begins with the magical words "I Can Read!"

*Visit www.icanread.com for information
on enriching your child's reading experience.*

I Can Read Book® is a trademark of HarperCollins Publishers.

Fancy Nancy: Chez Nancy
Copyright © 2018 by Disney Enterprises, Inc.
All rights reserved. Printed in the United States of America.
No part of this book may be used or reproduced in any manner whatsoever without written permission except in the case of brief quotations embodied in critical articles and reviews. For information address HarperCollins Children's Books, a division of HarperCollins Publishers, 195 Broadway, New York, NY 10007.
www.icanread.com

ISBN 978-0-06-279825-1

Book design by Scott Petrower

20 21 22   LSCC   10   ❖   First Edition

I Can Read!

BEGINNING 1 READING

Disney

Fancy NANCY

Chez Nancy

Adapted by Nancy Parent
Based on the episode
"Chez Nancy"
by Krista Tucker

Illustrations by the
Disney Storybook
Art Team

HARPER
An Imprint of HarperCollinsPublishers

Bonjour! My name is Nancy.

I'm excited to see

my fancy new playhouse.

I'm planning a party to celebrate.

Bree and I invite our friends.

"Come see my playhouse," I say.

"It's *ooh la la* fancy!"

Here comes Grace.

"I have a playhouse too," she says.

"Mine has a swing,

and mine has a slide."

7

"My playhouse is lavish," I say.

That's a fancy word for fancy.

"It has a fountain

and butterfly doors."

"It's more like a play palace," I say.

"We'll see about that," says Grace.

She rides away on her bike.

Bree and I head home.

"Will your playhouse really have

all that fancy stuff?" Bree asks.

"Yes! I told my dad

exactly what I wanted," I say.

I will see my playhouse at last!

Dad and Grandpa hold up a big sheet.

"One, two, ta-da!" says Dad.

Bree and I look at the playhouse.

I am confused.

"This is not fancy," I say.

"Your taste is a little too fancy
for our building skills," Dad says.

Bree and I go inside.

"This is not fancy," I say.

It's not at all like I imagined.

Where is the fountain?

Where are the butterfly doors?

I can't let Grace see this!

I have an idea.

"We'll make it fancy," I say.

"We'll make it a play palace!"

But our guests will be here soon.

I ask my little sister, JoJo,

and her friend Freddy to help.

They say yes!

We hurry and scurry.

We fix and fluff.

We make it *ooh la la* fancy.

JoJo and Freddy make

a fountain by the front door.

Voilà! Fancy!

My playhouse is ready.

Our friends arrive.

Grace looks all around.

She doesn't say a word.

JoJo and Freddy come inside.

They take all the snacks.

"Your playhouse would be fancy
if you didn't have to share it
with them," says Grace.
"My playhouse is all mine."

Maybe Grace is right.

"My playhouse is for big kids only,"
I tell JoJo.

JoJo looks really sad!

I smile at her.

"I need you to go back to your ship
and protect us from pirates!"

"Now that they're gone,

this place is perfect," says Grace.

This feels all wrong!

JoJo and Freddy helped

when I needed them.

They just wanted to play with us.

I change my mind . . .

Everyone is welcome!

"I'm sorry," I say to JoJo.

I ask JoJo and Freddy to come back.

I hope Grace will stay

and play with everyone.

But she decides to go home.

I go back to the party
with JoJo and Freddy.
I look around at all my friends
having fun together.

30

"I have the best playhouse ever,
because it has all of you," I say.

Fancy Nancy's Fancy Words

These are the fancy words in this book:

Chez— house of

Ooh la la— wow

Bonjour— hello

Lavish— fancy

Palace— a big, grand

house

Voilà— look at that

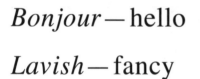